JUNGLE DAY

JUNGLE DAY

or, How I Learned to Love My Nosey Little Brother

written and illustrated by
BARBARA BOTTNER

Delacorte Press · New York

Published by
Delacorte Press
1 Dag Hammarskjold Plaza
New York, New York 10017

For Jeffrey

Manufactured in the United States of America

First printing

Library of Congress Cataloging in Publication Data

Bottner, Barbara.
Jungle day.

SUMMARY: With little brother's help Jackie composes
a totally new animal for Jungle Day at school.
[1. Brothers and sisters–Fiction]   I. Title.
PZ7.B6586 Ju   [E]   77-72645
ISBN 0-440-04383-2
ISBN 0-440-04384-0 lib. bdg.

The most important thing in Miss Naomi's class is Jungle Day. Everybody has to bring a cutout jungle animal. I can't draw, and there's nobody to help me except Wayne. But he's too little.

"Hey, Jackie, what are you making?" he asks.
"Maybe I could help you."

"If that's a camel, you forgot the hump," he says.

"Wayne, this happens to be a zebra without stripes."

"Do you want me to put in the stripes?" he asks.
"You're too little to put in these stripes," I tell him.

"How come you don't draw like Margaret Hooper?" he asks.

"Because she takes lessons, dummy. Today I have to draw something better than she does, otherwise she'll make fun of me."

"Wow! You've got a real cobra snake! Can I draw the fang?" asks Wayne.

"Wayne, this happens to be an alligator. Certain little brothers don't know how to go away."

"Can't I do anything?" he asks.

"Listen, Wayne, if you keep asking me dumb questions, I'll ask you one: Why couldn't I have an older brother who could help me, instead of a younger brother who's a pest?"

"But I am trying to help," he says.

Then Wayne yells: "You did it! You made a dinosaur! Yippee! Can I put in the fire and the smoke?"

"Definitely not. Because this isn't a dinosaur. It happens to be a hippopotamus."

"I've had enough of Jungle Day," I tell Wayne. "Margaret Hooper always makes fun of me. Last week she said my princess looked like a pumpkin head. I'm quitting!"

"Well, here comes Hooper with a lion, a safari jacket, and a mean look on her face," he says.

"What is that mess gonna be?" asks Hooper.

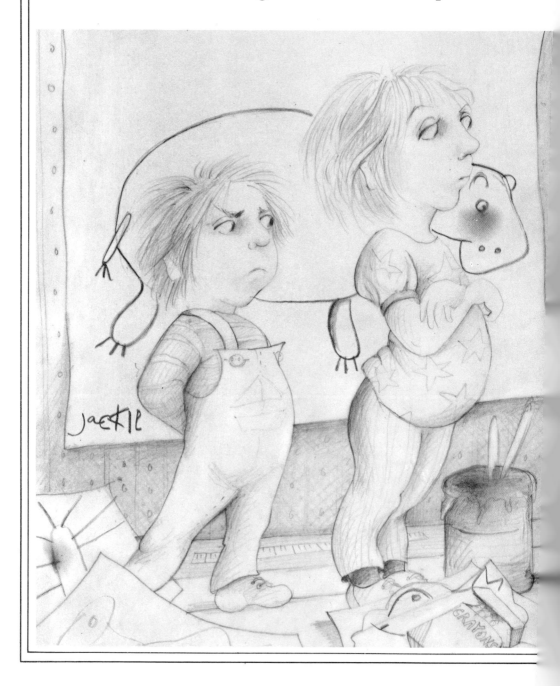

"You ought to punch out Margaret Hooper," whispers Wayne.

"Listen, Margaret," I tell her. "Our animal is one million years old, something you never even heard of. Just wait till you see it."

"Hah," says Hooper, "I've got the king of the jungle." And she walks away.

"You said our animal," Wayne yells. "Does that mean you're finally going to let *me* help?"

"Well, maybe. Got any ideas?"

"How about clay? We could use our Christmas clay and make a squirrel," he says, jumping up and down.

"Squirrels are not jungle animals," I tell him, "and clay is out."

"We could paint the cardboard box and make an elephant," he says.

"Nope," I tell him. "There's nothing for the trunk."

"What about puppets, puppets?" he's yelling.

"I must have been crazy to think a baby brother could help."

"Well," Wayne yells, "If I were you I would cut up all the animals that don't look like what they're supposed to look like, paste the best parts together, and make something nobody's ever seen before. That's what I would do."

Then he leaves my room.

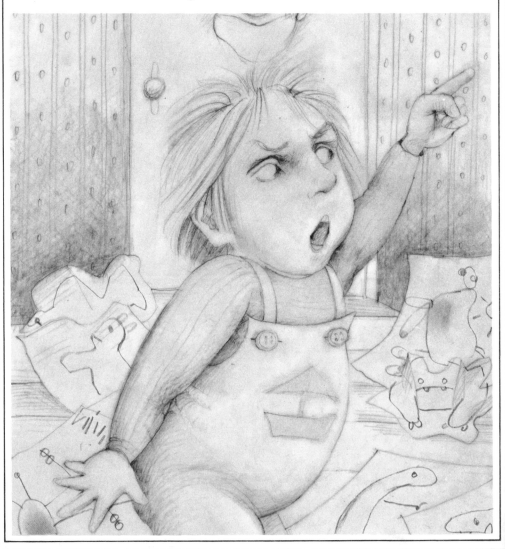

But he never leaves my room unless I kick him out,
I think to myself. So that's when I know he has a
good idea.

"Well, I can't do it by myself," I yell.

"What are you shouting about?" says Wayne, walking in slow motion.

"I can't do it alone," I say quietly.

"But I'm too little to help."

"You're perfect to help," I tell him.

"I'll cut out the nose from the alligator," I tell him, "and you cut the legs from the zebra."

"*I'm* cutting the belly from the hippo," he says, "and *you* can cut the legs from the zebra."

"OK," I tell him.

So we cut out everything and paste it together. Wayne is a little sloppy, but I don't say anything.

"Well, what is it?" he asks when we're done.

"I don't know," I tell him. "But whatever it is,

there's never been anything like it before in the whole entire world!"

"Well, there's never been anybody like you before," says Wayne.

Sometimes, maybe little brothers are okay!

ABOUT THE AUTHOR/ARTIST

Barbara Bottner has been an elementary school teacher, an actress, a book reviewer, and an award-winning filmmaker and illustrator. Among her many credits are films made for *The Electric Company*. She has also written and illustrated several picture books. She grew up on Long Island and now lives in New York City. Ms. Bottner does have a younger brother.

ABOUT THE BOOK

The art for this book was prepared on frosted acetate with lead pencil. Overlays were also done on acetate with lead pencil. The art for the cover was drawn with pencil on acetate, and the color was done with ink.

This book has been designed by Lynn Braswell. The text has been set in 16 point Plantin Alphatype by Royal Composing Room. The book was printed by General Offset Co., Inc., and bound by Economy Bookbinding Corporation.